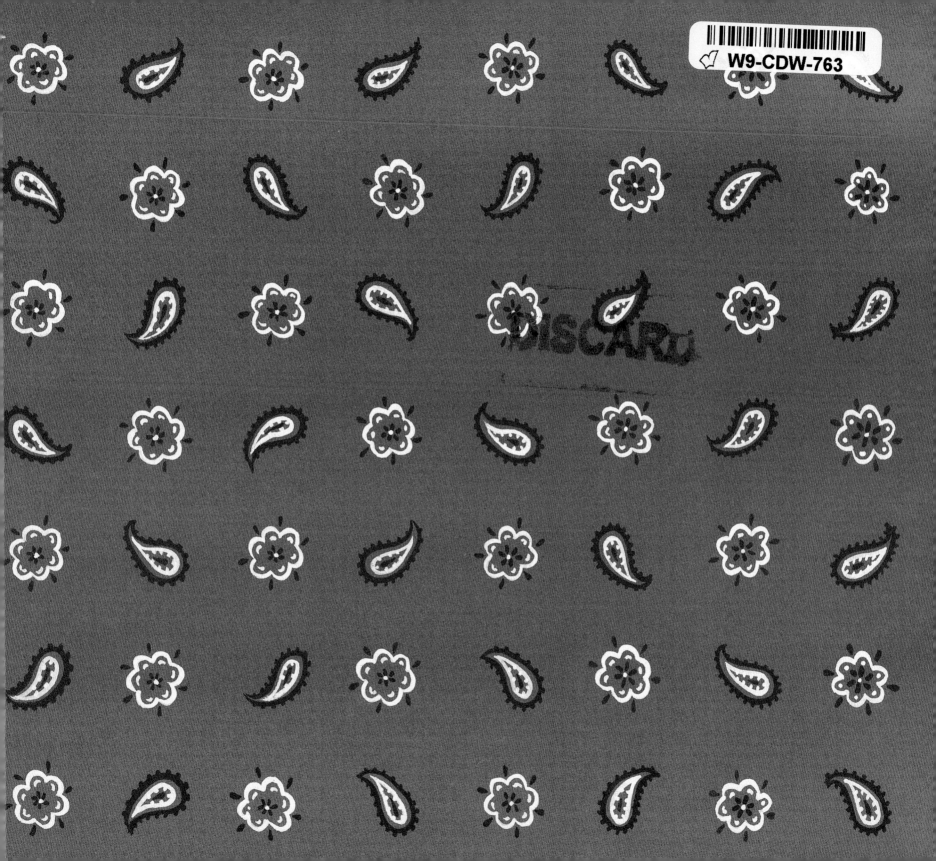

For Troy and his perfectly wonderful girls—K.A.

For Rosemary—J.M.

Text copyright © 2015 by Kathi Appelt • Illustrations copyright © 2015 by Jill McElmurry • All rights reserved. • For information about permission to reproduce selections from this book, write to Permissions, Houghton Mifflin Harcourt Publishing Company, 215 Park Avenue South, New York, New York 10003 • www.hmhco.com • The illustrations in this book were done in gouache on watercolor paper. • The text type was set in Graham. • The display type was set in Cactus Flower Solid. • Library of Congress Cataloging-in-Publication Data: Appelt, Kathi, 1954– When Otis courted Mama / Kathi Appelt; illustrated by Jill McElmurry. p. cm. Summary: While his life seems perfectly good as it is, Cardell, a young coyote, learns to tolerate—and even like—the coyote that is courting his mother. ISBN 978-0-15-216688-5 [1. Stepfathers—Fiction. 2. Mothers and sons—Fiction. 3. Fathers and sons—Fiction. 4. Coyote—Fiction.] I. McElmurry, Jill, ill. II. Title. PZ7.A6455 Wg 2014 [E]—dc22 2007029880 • Manufactured in China • SCP 10 9 8 7 6 5 4 3 2 1 • 4500497193

WHEN OTIS COURTED MAMA

KATHI APPELT

ILLUSTRATED BY

JILL McELMURRY

HOUGHTON MIFFLIN HARCOURT
Boston • New York

Before Otis, Cardell had a mostly wonderful life. He had a perfectly good mama and a perfectly good daddy. Both his perfectly good mama and his perfectly good daddy adored him. And Cardell adored them, too. With good reason.

Cardell's perfectly good daddy made the most fantastic jalapeño flapjacks, with just the right amount of saguaro syrup.

He was the master at playing Zig-the-Zag across the hot, burning sand, without leaving a single paw print.

Best of all, when his perfectly good daddy howled, the stars shimmered and the moon beamed. Cardell felt loved through and through.

The only problem was that Cardell's perfectly good daddy lived in a different part of the desert. Cardell had to share him with his perfectly nice stepmama, Lulu, and his perfectly cute stepbrother, Little Frankie. But Cardell was mostly used to it.

Besides, he only stayed there part of the time.
The rest of the time, he lived on the other side of
the desert, where he had his perfectly good mama
all to himself.

Cardell's mama was a champion scout. She knew how to hunt down pack rats and chuckwallas; even the sneakiest rattlesnakes couldn't hide from her. Cardell's tummy was always full.

She was also a master artist. She painted the most beautiful sunrises
and sunsets. Everyone agreed, her paintings were something to see.

Best of all, when his perfectly good
mama smiled, the moon, the stars, even the
planets glowed. Cardell felt warm and safe.
   Yep, apart from a few sticker burs and
occasional sand fleas, Cardell's life was
mostly wonderful.

But all of that was before Otis, their new neighbor, showed up at their door.

Otis came by their den just as the sun was setting, holding a handful of ocotillo flowers in one paw and a bag full of cactus candies in the other. Cardell felt a *grrr* form in his throat. But Mama seemed delighted.

Otis wasn't the first coyote to come courting Cardell's mama.
First there had been Cleburne, who was quite a dancer. He
and Mama danced all over the mesa. But the more Cleburne
danced, the more he slobbered.

"We can do without Cleburne," agreed Mama.

Moi, Moi, Moi!

Then there was Pierre, who played the accordion so sweetly that even the scorpions swooned. But talk about conceited! Cardell got tired of hearing Pierre talk about Pierre.

"Me too," said Mama.

Finally, there was Professor Coot. He was quite distinguished, but he was the expert on *everything*—the flowers, the rocks, the planets, even the sticker burs and sand fleas. Professor Coot was constantly correcting Cardell.

"Enough!" cried Mama.

But now . . . here was Otis.

Otis wasn't at all like Cleburne, Pierre, or Professor Coot. But he also wasn't like Cardell's perfectly good daddy. Otis couldn't make jalapeño flapjacks worth beans. When he played Zig-the-Zag, he left paw prints all over the hot, burning sand. And his howl sounded like he had rocks in the back of his throat.

Cardell expected his mama to say, "We can do without Otis." He waited and waited and waited. But "*Adiós, Otis*" never came.

So Cardell went on alert. His fur bristled. His ears lay back. His *GRRR* . . . got louder. He put Otis on notice.

A lesser coyote might have given up, but not Otis. He knew that Cardell was one tough little *hombre*. So, first, he stirred up a batch of prickly pear pudding. Cardell took a bite. His taste buds hummed. Yum!

It also turned out that Otis was a terrific pouncer. He pounced straight up into the air as if he had springs in his legs. Then he came back down fast as a shooting star. Cardell had to admit, he was somewhat impressed.

Nevertheless, Cardell kept expecting his mama
to say, *"Adiós, Otis."*

But when those words went unspoken, Cardell's
GRRR . . . stayed put.

Then one evening Otis told Cardell and Mama the funniest stories, stories about horned toads and chaparrals and little coyotes with big *GRRR*s . . . Cardell couldn't help it. He howled with laughter. Those stories settled on Cardell's fur like a warm blanket. Even the moon seemed to smile.

Before Otis left that night, he grabbed Cardell's paw and shook it, coyote to coyote. Cardell's *grrr* . . . got softer and softer and softer until it disappeared altogether.

A few moons later, Otis asked Mama to marry him.
Cardell—and Otis—waited and waited and waited. The
sun rose, the sun set, the stars shimmered in the desert sky.
Finally, all of the planets lined up just right. Then . . .

"Yes," Mama said at last. She smiled the biggest smile Cardell had ever seen. He looked at Otis, whose grin was just as wide. Then Mama and Otis both looked at Cardell, and he smiled right along with them.

After Otis, Cardell still had a perfectly good daddy and a perfectly good mama, a perfectly nice stepmama and a perfectly cute stepbrother. But now Cardell also had someone else: Otis!

And life? Sticker burs and sand fleas aside, it was mostly wonderful.